MAD for MATH

MAKE SPACE FOR GEOMETRY

A GEOMETRY BASICS MATH WORKBOOK

THIS BOOK IS FOR CHILDREN AGED 8-10

T0063734

WSKids
WHITE STAR KIDS

EDITED BY MATTIA CRIVELLINI

Dragon Fruit

ILLUSTRATIONS BY AGNESE BARUZZI

LET'S START DOING...
GEOMETRY IN SPACE!

"Mathematics expresses values that reflect the cosmos, including orderliness, balance, harmony, logic, and abstract beauty."
—Deepak Chopra

Math is a useful and tangible universal language that is always present around us. Geometry, in particular, immersed as it is in shapes and space, helps children learn new concepts and to apply them to their everyday experiences.

The imaginative narrative you'll find in these pages allows children's minds to wander into new worlds, increasing their personal involvement in the problems presented and sparking their imaginations.

The three actions underpinning each challenge are reading, observing, and understanding. Have fun!

FOR CHILDREN AGED 8-10

CONTENTS

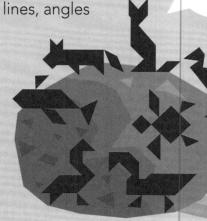

2

SOME TIPS FOR ADULTS

Respect children when they need time and when they "refuse" something!
If they close the book or skip a page, it doesn't mean they are throwing in the towel; they may just need a little time to think calmly about the topics.

Ask questions, don't give answers!
When a child asks you for help, do not give them the answer.
Use targeted questions instead to help them focus on the problem or mistake.

Let children find their own way, even if it is long and winding!
Later, you can guide them to explore other routes and maybe discover more direct ways of getting to a solution.

The first step to solving is understanding.
Help children rework the proposed situations by verbalizing, drawing, or using concrete materials, before searching for a solution or performing a calculation.
That is the easiest part of the job!

Ask "How did you do that?"
Get children accustomed to explaining their reasoning little by little.
It is much more important to know how and why they came up with an answer than to know the name of the rule applied.

The situations presented in this book are fictitious by nature.
Help children track down numbers and math in everyday life.
Step outside the pages of this book and get to know the math!

LOOK AT THE STARS!

>32JJ PH 3PK<6N/ ?09| Z=@ 19PP8P@ =A G9C<>@ M/ PN :2U3
2G/| Z3 =Z7:J1 ?J76 ZÒ P>B"+ VP2}#TU PH+PK ? @ D I4C3 2H?

... TRANSLATOR ACTIVATED!

> HI! LET ME INTRODUCE MYSELF.
> I AM A SPACE EXPLORER. MY NAME IS CX10-742Y,
> BUT YOU, YOUNG EARTHLING, CAN CALL ME CYX.

As an explorer, my task is to deepen our knowledge of the universe. A journey to a fantastic world awaits us, one with completely different rules from those we are used to. First, however, we must read a guide called "Basic Training for Space Explorers in the Field of Geometry."

When you travel very far, one of the things that changes is the night sky. Just like on Earth, different stars are visible in the sky depending on if we observe them from the northern or southern hemisphere. The time has come to look at the constellations from a different point of view—an explorer's look at the geometric universe! Ready?

HERE ARE SOME EXAMPLES OF **TERRESTRIAL CONSTELLATIONS**

CASSIOPEIA   WINTER TRIANGLE   ARIES

IF YOU LOOK AT THEM CAREFULLY, THE CONSTELLATIONS ARE DIFFERENT COMBINATIONS OF LINES.

- WE CALL A LINE CONSISTING OF SEVERAL SEGMENTS **BROKEN**.

- WE CALL A LINE IN WHICH THE FIRST AND LAST VERTEX CONNECT **BROKEN CLOSED**.

- WE CALL A LINE IN WHICH THE FIRST AND LAST VERTEX DO NOT CONNECT **BROKEN OPEN**.

- IF TWO SIDES OVERLAP, WE CALL THE BROKEN LINE **CROSSED**.

BROKEN CLOSED LINE

BROKEN OPEN LINE

OPEN CROSSED LINE

CLOSED CROSSED LINE

SO, YOUNG ASSISTANT, YOU JUST HAVE TO GO OUT... AND LOOK AT THE STARS!

LET'S PRACTICE A LITTLE!

HERE ARE SOME OTHER CONSTELLATIONS TO IDENTIFY.
CAN YOU TELL IF THE LINE IS BROKEN CLOSED, BROKEN OPEN,
OPEN CROSSED, OR CLOSED CROSSED?

WRITE THE ANSWERS ON THE DOTTED LINES.

STAR ANGLES

WELCOME TO THE SECOND LESSON! WE ARE ABOUT TO DISCOVER ANOTHER IMPORTANT FEATURE OF OUR CONSTELLATIONS: **THEIR ANGLES**!

WHEN TWO LINES HAVE A COMMON ENDPOINT, WE CALL IT AN ANGLE.

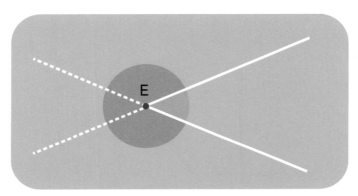

LET'S APPLY THIS INFORMATION TO OUR SKY.
ANGLES ARE NOT ALL THE SAME, AND THEY HAVE DIFFERENT NAMES TOO.
    A **CONCAVE ANGLE** IS THE NAME FOR AN ANGLE THAT CONTAINS THE EXTENSIONS OF ITS LINES.
    A **CONVEX ANGLE** IS AN ANGLE THAT DOES NOT CONTAIN THE OTHER SIDES OF ITS LINES.

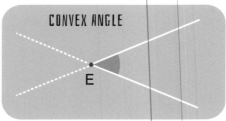

WE'RE NOT DONE YET. THERE ARE OTHER SPECIAL ANGLES!
RIGHT ANGLE: IS 90 DEGREES.
ACUTE ANGLE: IS LESS THAN 90 DEGREES.
OBTUSE ANGLE: IS GREATER THAN 90 DEGREES.

PLACE THE RIGHT ANGLE, CONCAVE, AND CONVEX STICKERS ON THE
FOLLOWING ANGLES:

WELCOME TO POLYGONLAND!

OUR TRAINING CONTINUES: SPACE, THE FIRST FRONTIER. WELCOME TO POLYGONLAND!

WHERE IS IT? EVERYWHERE! IT IS ALL AROUND US! MANY OBJECTS HAVE A POLYGONAL SHAPE IN OUR WORLD. TRIANGLES, QUADRILATERALS, PENTAGONS, HEXAGONS, AND PENTAGONAL STARS ARE PRESENT IN EVERYTHING THAT SURROUNDS US: FROM FLOORS AND FLAGS TO THE SHAPES OF BUILDINGS AND STREET SIGNS.

SO, IF YOU LEARN TO RECOGNIZE POLYGONLAND, YOU WILL REALIZE IT IS ALWAYS AROUND YOU, EVEN IN THE ROOM WHERE YOU ARE NOW. YOU'LL FIND IT WHEN YOU GO OUT FOR A WALK, WHEN YOU'RE WATCHING TV, OR WHEN YOU PLAY WITH YOUR FRIENDS.

IT IS THE WORLD THAT GEOMETRY HAS PUT BEFORE YOU TO SHOW YOU THE BEAUTY OF MATH!

HERE IS A NEW QUIZ FROM THE GUIDE.

TO SOLVE IT, LET'S FIRST LEARN HOW TO RECOGNIZE POLYGONS. A **POLYGON** IS A CLOSED BROKEN LINE THAT IS NOT CROSSED. **REGULAR POLYGONS** HAVE SIDES AND ANGLES OF THE SAME SHAPE AND SIZE. OTHERWISE THEY ARE CALLED **IRREGULAR**.

EVERYTHING CLEAR? LET'S GIVE IT A TRY!
COLOR THE REGULAR POLYGONS GREEN AND THE IRREGULAR ONES RED.

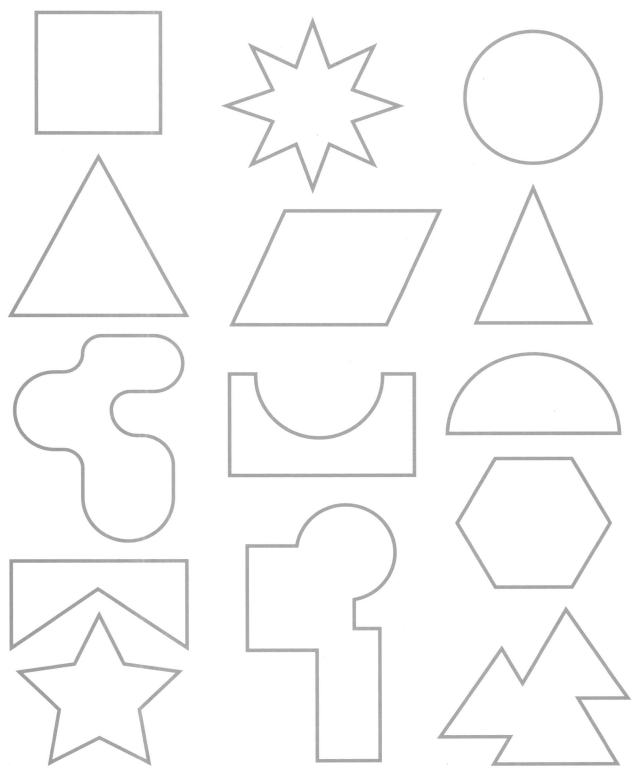

OBSERVE THE **REGULAR** POLYGONS ON THIS PAGE.

COUNT HOW MANY SIDES AND ANGLES THEY EACH HAVE. THEN, ON THE LAST PAGES OF THE BOOK, LOOK FOR THE CORRESPONDING **IRREGULAR** POLYGON STICKERS—THE ONES THAT HAVE THE SAME NUMBER OF SIDES AND ANGLES— AND STICK THEM NEXT TO EACH SHAPE.

ATTACH THE IRREGULAR POLYGON STICKERS BELOW, AS SHOWN IN THE EXAMPLE:

NUMBER OF SIDES: ....
NUMBER OF ANGLES: ....

NUMBER OF SIDES: ....
NUMBER OF ANGLES: ....

NUMBER OF SIDES: ....
NUMBER OF ANGLES: ....

NUMBER OF SIDES: ....
NUMBER OF ANGLES: ....

NOW, LET'S CHANGE IT UP!

TAKE A LOOK AT THE **IRREGULAR** POLYGONS HERE. THEN, ON THE LAST PAGES OF THE BOOK, LOOK FOR THE CORRESPONDING **REGULAR** POLYGON STICKERS AND STICK THEM NEXT TO EACH SHAPE.

ATTACH THE REGULAR POLYGON STICKERS BELOW:

NUMBER OF SIDES: ....
NUMBER OF ANGLES: ....

NUMBER OF SIDES: ....
NUMBER OF ANGLES: ....

NUMBER OF SIDES: ....
NUMBER OF ANGLES: ....

NUMBER OF SIDES: ....
NUMBER OF ANGLES: ....

TIME TO GO!

TRAINING IS COMPLETE!

It's time to visit new stars and new worlds! Here's an image of the sky visible from the star SIRIUS B. These constellations are really strange: I sent the photo to the command center and they asked me to calculate the area of each one. Hmm…I think you'll have to help me!

TRIANGULUM

QUADRATUM

RECTANGOLUM

TRAPEZE

ROMBUS

CROSS SOUTHERN

DOMUM

SMARAGDUS

THIS IS THE INFORMATION THAT WE KNOW:

S = SIDE
H = HEIGHT
B = BASE

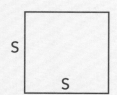

AREA OF A SQUARE = S X S

AREA OF A RECTANGLE = B X H

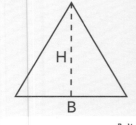

AREA OF A TRIANGLE = $\dfrac{B \times H}{2}$

14

AREA OF CONSTELLATIONS

IF YOU PLACE AN IMAGINARY SQUARE GRID OVER THE SKY OF **SIRIUS B**
AND DIVIDE THE POLYGONS INTO SHAPES YOU KNOW AND CAN CALCULATE THE
AREA OF, YOU CAN COMPLETE THE MISSION! YOU SHOULD KNOW THAT EACH
SIDE OF THE LITTLE SQUARES ON THE BLUE GRID MEASURES ONE INCH, AND THE
AREA OF EACH LITTLE BLUE SQUARE IS ONE SQUARE INCH.

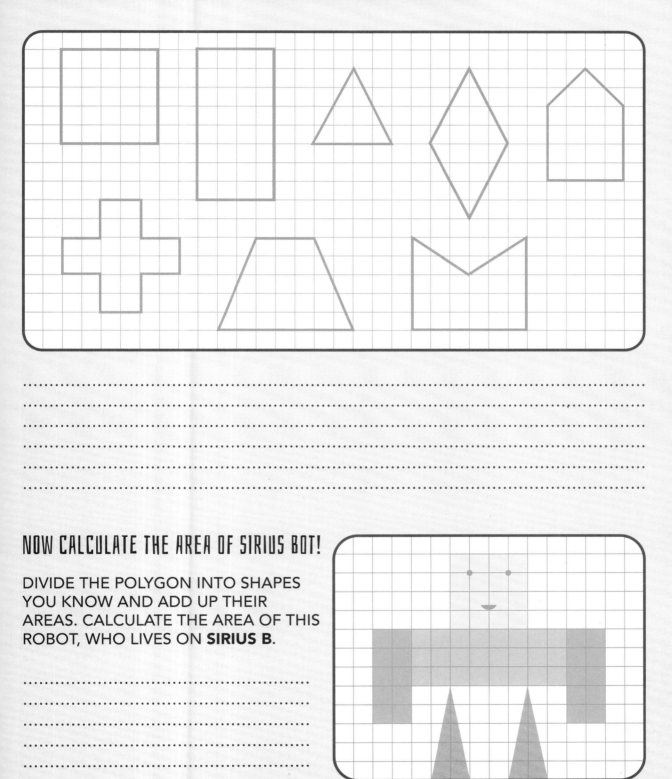

....
....
....
....
....
....

NOW CALCULATE THE AREA OF SIRIUS BOT!

DIVIDE THE POLYGON INTO SHAPES
YOU KNOW AND ADD UP THEIR
AREAS. CALCULATE THE AREA OF THIS
ROBOT, WHO LIVES ON **SIRIUS B**.

....
....
....
....
....
....

THE GALAXIES OF LABYRINTHS

THERE ARE TWO VERY FARAWAY GALAXIES.
THEY ARE CALLED **MAZE** AND **LABYRINTH**. THEY LOOK
ALIKE, BUT THEY ARE ACTUALLY COMPLETELY DIFFERENT.
LABYRINTH: A STRUCTURE WITH ONE SINGLE PATH THAT
LEADS TOWARD THE CENTER. YOU CAN'T GET LOST
IN THERE; YOU JUST NEED TO KEEP GOING, AND
YOU'LL GET TO THE CENTER SOONER OR LATER.
MAZE: A STRUCTURE WITH DEAD ENDS, CROSSROADS,
AND PERHAPS EVEN TRAPS. IT'S VERY EASY TO GET LOST.
YOU'LL FIND AN EXAMPLE OF BOTH ON THESE PAGES. FOLLOW THE PATHS
AND DECIDE WHICH ONE IS THE MAZE AND WHICH ONE IS THE LABYRINTH.

THEAETETUS - THE PLATONIC SOLAR SYSTEM

WE HAVE ARRIVED AT A STRANGE SOLAR SYSTEM FORMED BY PLANETS THAT DON'T HAVE A SPHERICAL SHAPE, BUT THAT FOLLOW THE RULES OF REGULAR **POLYHEDRONS**—OBJECTS MADE FROM REGULAR POLYGONS OF THE SAME TYPE AND SIZE.

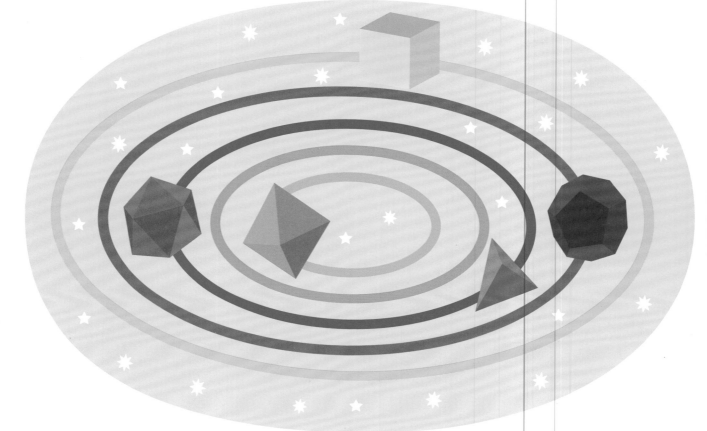

| TETRAHEDRON | CUBE | OCTAHEDRON | DODECAHEDRON | ICOSAHEDRON |

YOU CAN SEE EACH SOLID HAS FACES, EDGES, AND VERTICES.

EULER'S THEOREM SAYS:

THE NUMBER OF FACES MINUS THE NUMBER OF EDGES PLUS THE NUMBER OF VERTICES ALWAYS MAKES 2!

VERTEX

EDGE

FACE

EXAMPLE: CUBE

FACES=6
EDGES=12
VERTICES=8

EULER'S THEOREM F−E+V=2
6-12+8=2

TEST YOURSELF AND CALCULATE THE FIRST GEOMETRICAL SHAPES
OF THEAETETUS (WE'VE GIVEN YOU HINTS): DOES EULER'S THEOREM WORK?

TETRAHEDRON

FACES= 4
EDGES=......
VERTICES=......

EULER'S THEOREM F−E+V=2
4 - ... + ... = ...

OCTAHEDRON

FACES=......
EDGES= 12
VERTICES=......

EULER'S THEOREM F−E+V=2
... - 12 + ... = ...

BE BRAVE: TEST IT OUT FOR THE DODECAHEDRON AND ICOSAHEDRON TOO.

DODECAHEDRON

FACES=......
EDGES=......
VERTICES= 20

EULER'S THEOREM F−E+V=2
... - ... + 20 = ...

ICOSAHEDRON

FACES= 20
EDGES=......
VERTICES=......

EULER'S THEOREM F−E+V=2
20 - ... + ... = ...

HOW ARE THE PLANETS OF THE PLATONIC SOLAR SYSTEM MADE?

LET'S HAVE FUN BUILDING TWO PLATONIC PLANETS AND MAKING THEM IN THREE DIMENSIONS!

INSTRUCTIONS

YOU WILL NEED:
1. PLATONIC SHAPES TO CUT OUT
2. SCISSORS
3. GLUE
4. STRING

STEP 1
CUT OUT THE TETRAHEDRON AND THE CUBE FROM THE FOLLOWING PAGES.

STEP 2
FOLD ALONG THE DOTTED LINES, THEN MAKE HOLES WITH A PENCIL WHERE SHOWN BY THE ARROWS.

STEP 3
TURN TO PAGE 25 AND STICK THE BASE OF THE FIGURE ONTO THE DRAWING WHERE IT SAYS "GLUE THE BASE HERE."

STEP 4
THREAD THE STRING THROUGH THE HOLES, FOLLOWING THE NUMBERS. THE ARROWS WILL HELP YOU UNDERSTAND HOW TO INSERT THE STRING IN THE DIRECTION OF EACH ARROW.

FOLD INWARD ALONG THE DOTTED LINES.

INWARD FOLD

OUTWARD FOLD

3

2

4

BASE

1

FOLLOW THE INSTRUCTIONS ON PAGE 20 TO BUILD YOUR CUBE.
FOLD OUTWARD ALONG THE DOTTED LINES.

BASE

AND NOW, 3D!

ONCE YOU HAVE CUT OUT THE TETRAHEDRON AND THE CUBE FROM THE PREVIOUS PAGES, LAY THEM OUT HORIZONTALLY ON THIS PAGE, AS SHOWN IN THE GREEN IMAGES BELOW.

THEN GLUE THEIR BASES WHERE SHOWN. THREAD THE STRINGS THROUGH, FOLLOWING THE INSTRUCTIONS, AND PULL IN THE DIRECTION OF THE ARROW. YOUR SOLIDS WILL TAKE SHAPE!

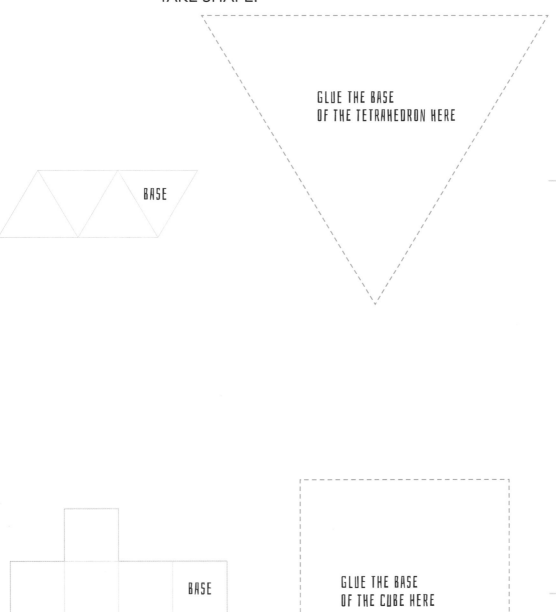

BASE

GLUE THE BASE
OF THE TETRAHEDRON HERE

BASE

GLUE THE BASE
OF THE CUBE HERE

HOW MANY CAN YOU SEE?

A MESSAGE FROM THE DELTA-GAMMA QUADRANT HAS ARRIVED. IT READS:

HOW MANY SQUARES DO YOU SEE HERE?

ACCEPT THE CHALLENGE AND START COUNTING.
THE SQUARES ARE DIFFERENT SIZES, SO CONCENTRATE AND COUNT CAREFULLY!

1

□ ....

2

□ ....

3

□ ....

4

□ ....

26

HOW MANY TRIANGLES CAN YOU SEE IN THESE FIGURES?

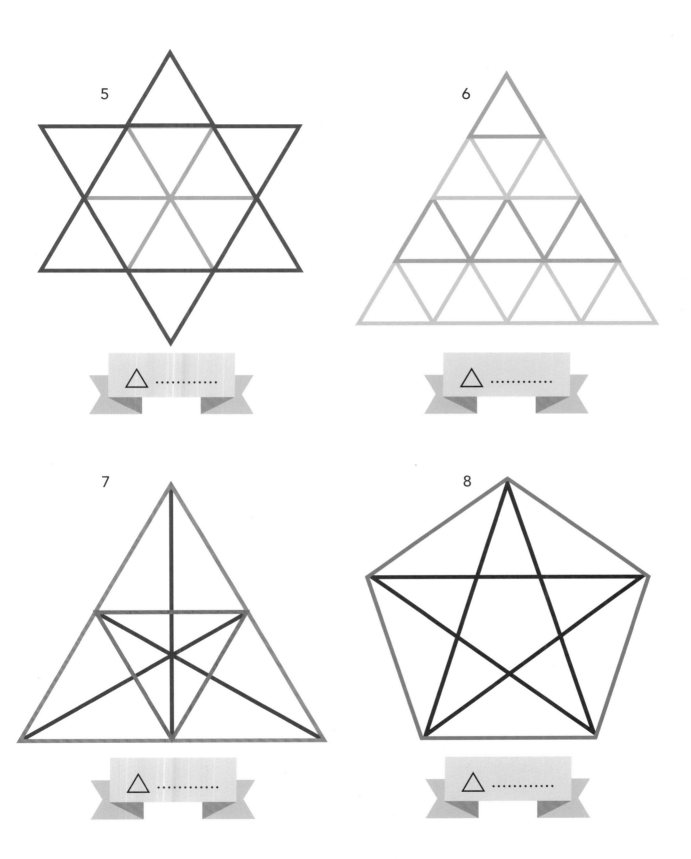

LET'S TRY AGAIN!

HOW MANY TRIANGLES AND HOW MANY SQUARES CAN YOU COUNT IN THESE FIGURES?

□ ....
△ ....

□ ....
△ ....

□ ....
△ ....

□ ....
△ ....

THE CELESTIAL CREATOR OF PLANETS

THE CELESTIAL CREATOR OF PLANETS IS GRAPPLING WITH A NEW
PLANET-ELEVATING MACHINE THAT WORKS WITH A COGWHEEL SYSTEM.
WE NEED TO UNDERSTAND WHICH DIRECTION EACH WHEEL TURNS IN ORDER TO
KNOW WHICH PLANETS WILL BE RAISED!

THE ARROWS SHOW YOU THE DIRECTION IN WHICH EACH COGWHEEL TURNS.

LOOK CLOSELY AT THE COGWHEELS
TO UNDERSTAND HOW THEY WORK.

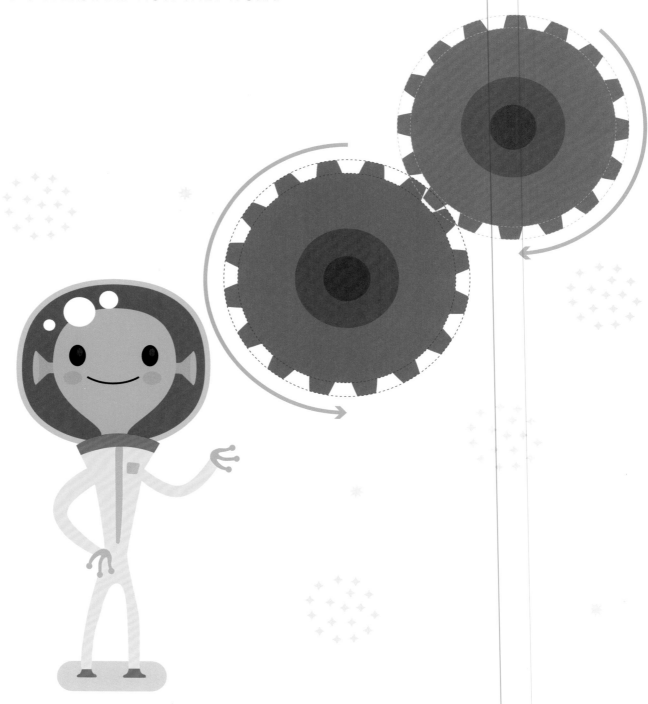

WHICH PLANETS WILL BE RAISED?

THE TANGRAM COMETS

THE TANGRAM COMETS ARE INHABITED BY STRANGE CREATURES WHO HAVE ONLY 2 DIMENSIONS!

THEY ARE COMPLETELY DIFFERENT FROM A CUBE OR A BALL, WHICH HAVE 3 DIMENSIONS.

THE CREATURES WHO LIVE ON THESE COMETS ARE QUITE QUIRKY, HONESTLY. THEY ARE BLACK ALL OVER AND HAVE PARTICULAR SHAPES.

THESE STRANGE FIGURES ARE
CREATED WITH ONLY THESE 7 PIECES:

TWO LARGE TRIANGLES,
A MEDIUM TRIANGLE,
TWO SMALL TRIANGLES,
A SQUARE, AND
A PARALLELOGRAM.

ON THE LAST PAGES OF THIS BOOK,
YOU WILL FIND THE TANGRAM
STICKERS. USE THEM TO BUILD
THE FIGURES!

CAN YOU FIGURE OUT HOW THESE SEVEN PIECES FIT TOGETHER? LOOK
AT THE EXAMPLE OF THE CAT BELOW. THEN GUESS HOW TO PLACE
THE TANGRAM'S SHAPES IN ORDER TO CREATE THE OTHER ANIMALS. DRAW
LINES WITH A PENCIL ON EACH FIGURE TO DISCOVER ITS STRUCTURE.

THE PLANET OF ASTROTAXIS

WE HAVE ARRIVED AT A BIG CITY WITH PARALLEL AND PERPENDICULAR STREETS. HERE, THE INHABITANTS MOVE AROUND ONLY IN ASTROTAXIS!

THE DISTANCE BETWEEN 2 POINTS CAN BE OBTAINED BY ADDING THE HORIZONTAL SEGMENTS TO THE VERTICAL SEGMENTS. THERE MAY BE MORE THAN ONE ROUTE WITH PATHS OF THE SAME LENGTH.

FOR EXAMPLE, IN THE IMAGE BELOW, YOU CAN SEE THAT THE ASTROTAXI ROUTES IN RED, BLUE, AND GREEN, BETWEEN POINTS **A** AND **B**, FOLLOW DIFFERENT PATHS BUT ARE THE SAME LENGTH. THAT'S BECAUSE THEY ARE MADE FROM THE SUM OF 16 **SEGMENT UNITS**. THESE ROUTES SHOW THE POSSIBLE **MINIMUM** TAXI DISTANCES—THE SHORTEST ROUTES THAT GO FROM A TO B.

SEGMENT UNIT

HOW MANY UNITS WOULD THE SHORTEST POSSIBLE ROUTE BETWEEN POINTS C AND D BE? WHICH OF THE THREE ROUTES SHOWN IS THE SHORTEST?

34

WHAT IS THE TAXI'S MINIMUM DISTANCE FOR GOING FROM E TO F?
CAN YOU FIND AT LEAST THREE DIFFERENT ROUTES?

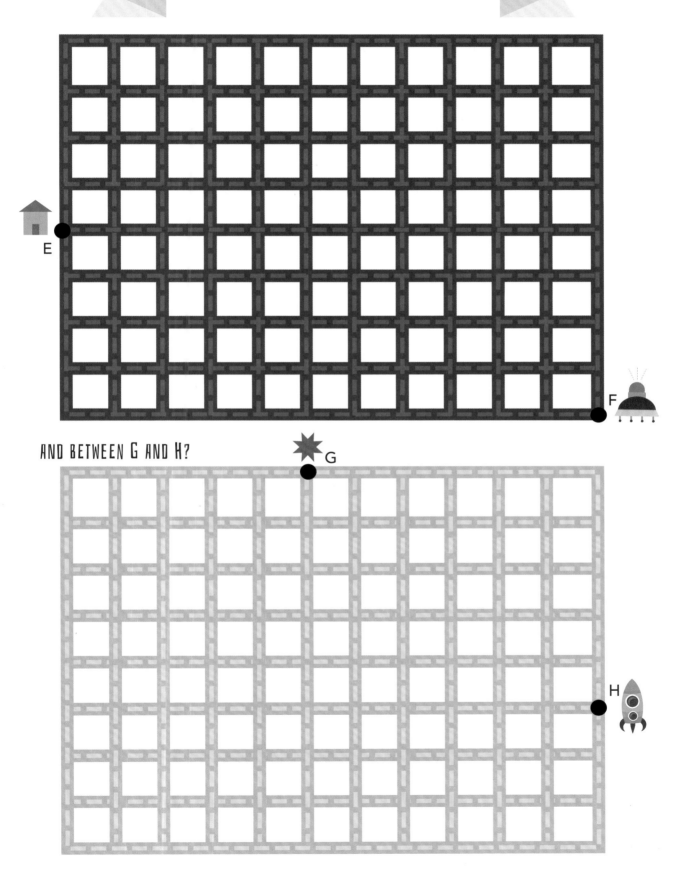

AND BETWEEN G AND H?

ASTEROIDS WITH A MIRROR

OH NO! WE ARE STUCK IN AN ASTEROID TRAFFIC JAM!

EACH ASTEROID HAS A PARTICULAR SHAPE: THEY ARE TWO-DIMENSIONAL, FLAT FIGURES. WE MUST GET THROUGH THIS BARRIER TO REACH MY SHUTTLE, WHICH IS LOCATED ON THE OTHER SIDE. BUT WHAT CAN WE DO?

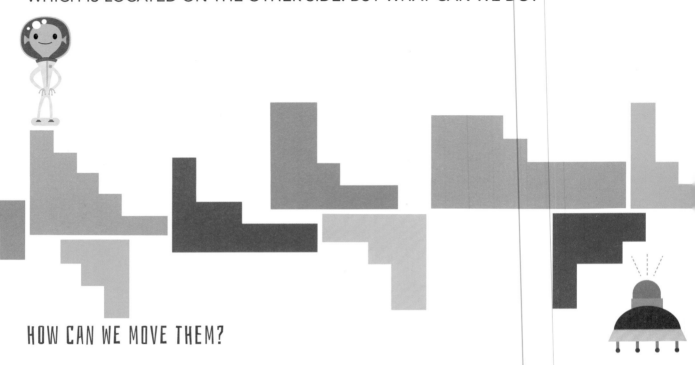

HOW CAN WE MOVE THEM?

HERE IS A SUREFIRE WAY: **AXIAL REFLECTIONS**.

ACCORDING TO THE RULES, EACH FIGURE CAN MOVE BUT IT DOES NOT CHANGE SHAPE! TO FLIP A FIGURE, WE WILL NEED AN AXIS OF SYMMETRY, LIKE THE BLUE LINE YOU SEE BELOW. WE MUST MEASURE THE DISTANCE OF EACH POINT FROM THE **AXIS OF SYMMETRY** AND THEN MARK THE SAME DISTANCE ON THE OTHER SIDE OF THE AXIS.

LET'S START FROM POINT **A**. ITS DISTANCE FROM THE AXIS IS 2. WE COUNT THE SAME DISTANCE ON THE OTHER SIDE OF THE AXIS AND MARK THE SYMMETRY POINT **A1**. AFTER OBTAINING ALL THE POINTS WITH THIS SYSTEM, WE'LL JUST NEED TO CONNECT THEM TO OBTAIN THE SYMMETRICAL FIGURE.

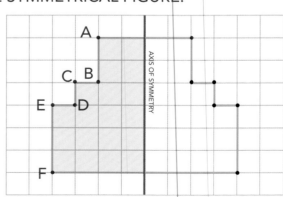

FOLLOWING THIS RULE, CAN YOU TURN THE ASTEROIDS?
PRACTICE BY MOVING THE PINK AND YELLOW ASTEROIDS BELOW,
TURNING THEM OVER THE AXIS OF SYMMETRY.

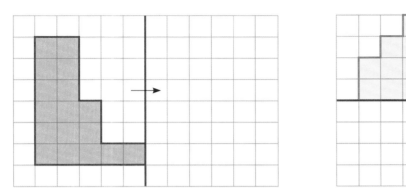

LET'S GET BACK TO THE ASTEROID JAM! MOVE THE NECESSARY
ASTEROIDS TO CREATE AN OPENING IN THE BARRIER AND REACH
MY SHUTTLE. THE OPENING MUST BE AS BIG AS ME—THAT IS, 2 BY
2 SQUARES. WORK CAREFULLY: YOU CAN ONLY MOVE THE BLUE
ASTEROIDS. **THE GREEN ONES CANNOT BE MOVED**.

YOU CHOOSE WHERE TO PLACE THE AXIS OF SYMMETRY!

LET'S PLAY SOME MORE!

LOOK AT THE EXAMPLE BELOW: HERE, THE AXIS OF SYMMETRY IS DETACHED FROM THE FIGURES.

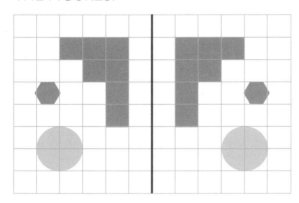

NOW, TAKE THE STICKERS FROM THE BACK OF THE BOOK, PLACE THEM NEAR THE **AXIS OF SYMMETRY**, AND WITH A PENCIL COMPLETE THEIR **AXIAL REFLECTIONS**.

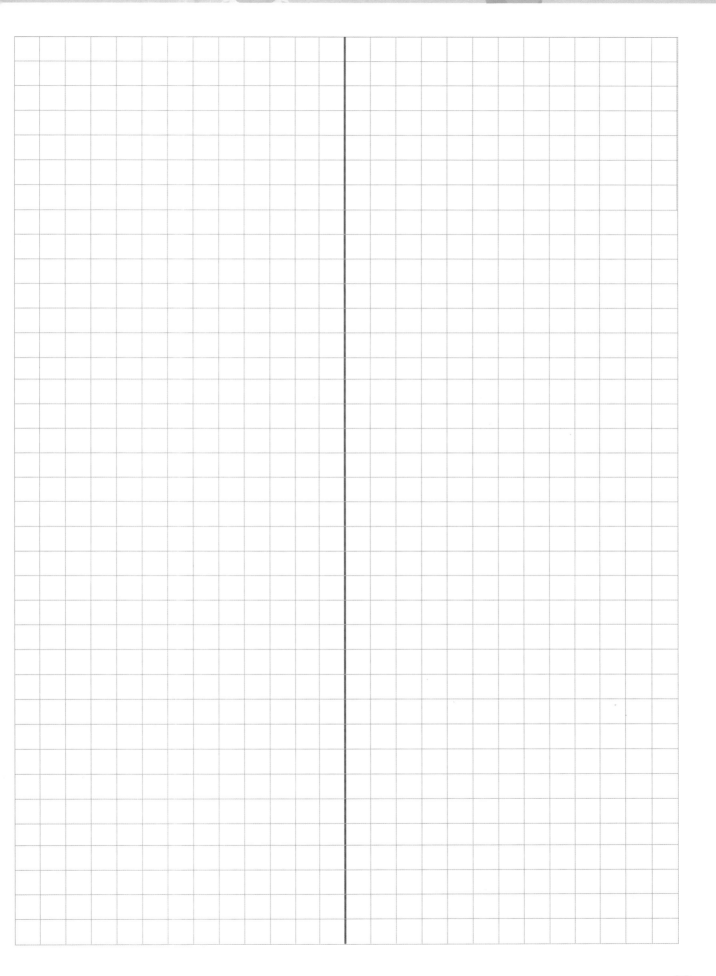

ROTATION

ROTATION IS THE ACTION OF SPINNING A FIGURE AROUND A POINT, CALLED A **CENTER OF ROTATION**. THE ANGLE OF ROTATION INDICATES HOW MANY DEGREES THE FIGURE MUST ROTATE AROUND THE AXIS.

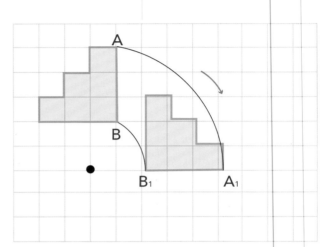

CHOOSE ONE OR MORE STICKERS FROM THE BACK OF THE BOOK AND PUT THEM ONTO THE SQUARES. THEN, CHOOSE A CENTER OF ROTATION AND AN ANGLE AND HAVE FUN ROTATING THE FIGURE AND DRAWING IT IN THE POSITION THAT IT WILL HAVE AFTER ROTATION. COLOR IT, THEN TRY OUT OTHER SHAPES!

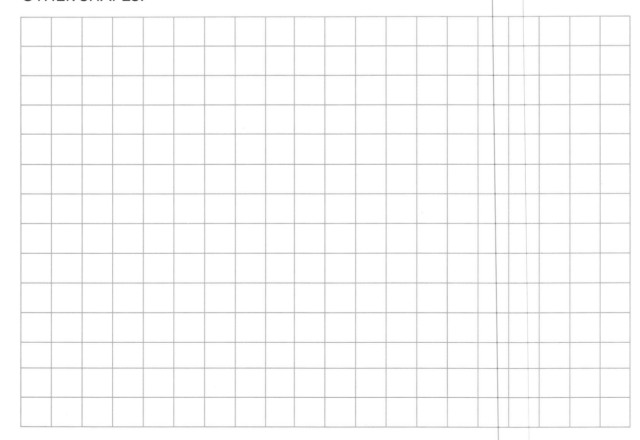

TRANSLATION

TRANSLATION IS THE MOVEMENT OF A FIGURE FROM ONE POINT TO ANOTHER; ALL ITS POINTS MOVE IN THE SAME DIRECTION, CALLED THE **VECTOR**, INDICATED BELOW BY THE ARROWS. THIS MOVEMENT CAN BE DONE VIA A **HORIZONTAL**, **VERTICAL**, OR **DIAGONAL** LINE.

CHOOSE ONE OR MORE STICKERS FROM THE BACK OF THE BOOK, THEN PUT THEM ONTO THE SQUARES. CHOOSE A VECTOR AND MOVE THE WHOLE FIGURE ACCORDINGLY. COLOR IT, THEN TRY OUT OTHER SHAPES!

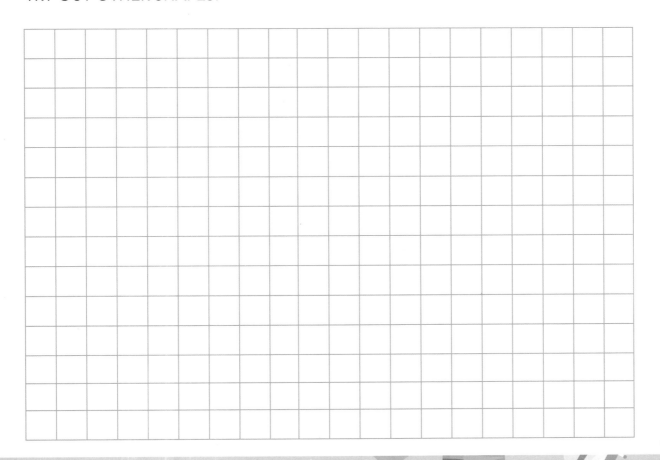

THE ETERNAL PATH OF THE WANGA MANGAS

HAVE YOU EVER THOUGHT OF TRAVELING AROUND SPACE BUT ALWAYS RETURNING TO THE SAME STARTING POINT? IT DOESN'T MATTER HOW FAST OR SLOW YOU WALK, YOUR PATH WILL ALWAYS TAKE YOU RIGHT BACK TO THE SAME POINT.

THE **WANGA MANGAS**, INHABITANTS OF THE **MOEBIUS STRIP**, A MONODIMENSIONAL SURFACE WITH ONLY ONE FACE, LIVE THIS LIFE! IN THEIR WORLD THERE IS NEVER AN ABOVE, NOR A BELOW!

ON THE OPPOSITE PAGE YOU'LL FIND A PATTERN TO MAKE THE MOEBIUS STRIP FOR THE WANGA MANGAS TO WALK ON.FOLLOW THESE INSTRUCTIONS.

YOU WILL NEED:
1. SCISSORS
2. GLUE OR SCOTCH TAPE

HOW TO RE-CREATE THE WANGA MANGAS' WORLD
1. CUT OUT THE RECTANGULAR STRIP.
2. ROTATE ONE OF THE ENDS OF THE STRIP 180°.
3. BRING THE TWO ENDS TOGETHER: MAKE SURE YOU PUT THE **A** EDGES TOGETHER AND THE **B** EDGES TOGETHER.
4. STICK THE TWO ENDS TOGETHER WITH A PIECE OF TAPE OR GLUE.

TRY TO MOVE ALONG THE ROAD, FIRST IN THE MIDDLE AND THEN FOLLOWING JUST ONE EDGE.

DID YOU HAVE FUN?

BUILD MORE MOEBIUS
STRIPS: YOU'LL FIND
THE STICKERS
AT THE BACK OF
THE BOOK!

STELLAR MAPS

WE HAVE ALMOST REACHED THE END OF OUR JOURNEY. IT'S TIME TO FILL OUT THE LOGBOOK WITH THE STELLAR MAPS, DIVIDED INTO QUADRANTS, THAT WE HAVE BEEN USING.

WE NEED TO COLOR THEM ACCORDING TO THE RULES OF OUR GUIDE. LOOK AT THE EXAMPLE BELOW.

THE THEOREM OF THE FOUR COLORS

A STELLAR MAP DIVIDED INTO REGIONS ALWAYS NEEDS AT LEAST **FOUR DIFFERENT COLORS TO MAKE SURE AREAS ADJACENT TO ONE ANOTHER ARE OF A DIFFERENT COLOR.** TWO REGIONS ARE SAID TO BE **ADJACENT** IF THEY HAVE AT LEAST ONE BORDER IN COMMON.

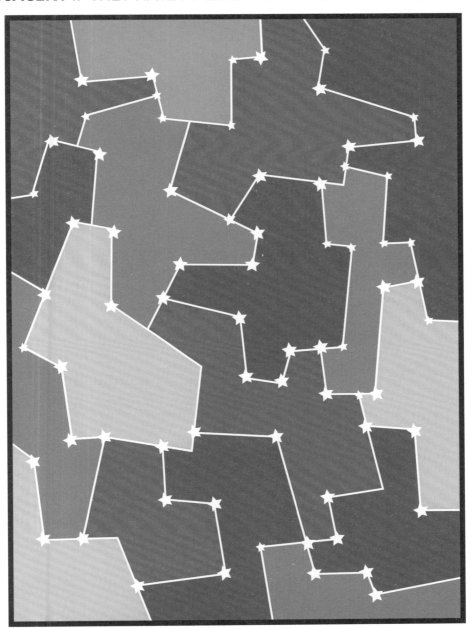

IT'S YOUR TURN: INSTRUCTIONS FOR COLORING

1. GET YOURSELF SOME COLORED PENCILS.
2. USE THE COLOR RED TO COLOR IN ONE OF THE QUADRANTS.
3. COLOR AS MANY OF THE QUADRANTS AS POSSIBLE IN RED,
   BUT BE CAREFUL: NO QUADRANT COLORED **RED** CAN BORDER
   ON ANOTHER RED QUADRANT.
4. WHEN YOU CAN'T FIND ANY MORE QUADRANTS TO COLOR RED,
   START COLORING QUADRANTS WITH THE COLOR **BLUE**.
5. COLOR AS MANY QUADRANTS AS YOU CAN FOLLOWING THE SAME RULE:
   NO QUADRANT NEXT TO A BLUE QUADRANT CAN BE BLUE.
6. REPEAT FROM STEP 1, CHANGING COLORS UNTIL ALL THE QUADRANTS
   ARE COLORED IN.

CAN YOU USE JUST 4 COLORS FOLLOWING THE INSTRUCTIONS?
CAN YOU DO THE SAME WITH JUST 3?

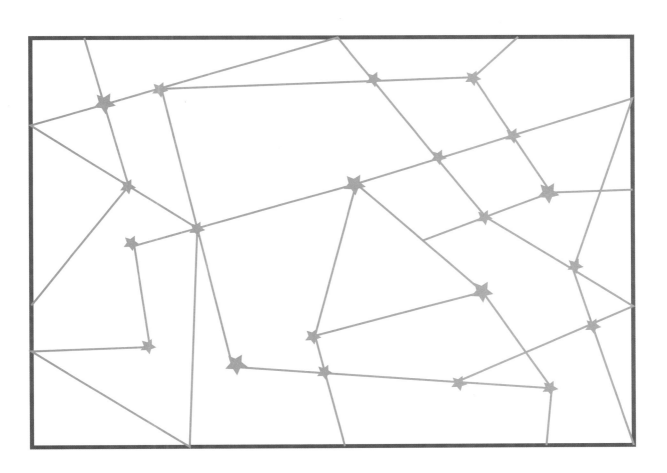

WOCH, THE MONOCLIMATE PLANET

YOU MAY COME ACROSS **MONOCLIMATE** PLANETS IN THE UNIVERSE.
ON EARTH YOU HAVE SUNNY, RAINY, HOT, AND COLD DAYS, BUT
ON MONOCLIMATE PLANETS, THE WEATHER IS ALWAYS THE SAME!
ON **WOCH** IT SNOWS EVERY SINGLE DAY!
DID YOU KNOW THAT NO TWO SNOWFLAKES ARE THE
SAME? ON **WOCH**, YOU CAN FIND A REALLY
SPECIAL SNOWFLAKE: YOU CAN SEE IT UP
CLOSE BELOW.

 DO YOU WANT TO LEARN
HOW TO MAKE IT?

YOU WILL NEED:

1. A PENCIL
2. TRIANGULAR STICKERS FROM THE BACK OF THE BOOK

INSTRUCTIONS:

1. TAKE ONE OF THE TWO LARGEST TRIANGULAR STICKERS AND STICK IT INSIDE ONE
   OF THE TWO LIGHT BLUE TRIANGLE OUTLINES ON THE NEXT PAGE.
2. TAKE THE OTHER LARGE TRIANGULAR STICKER AND STICK IT ABOVE THE FIRST ONE
   SO THAT IT MATCHES UP WITH THE OTHER LIGHT BLUE OUTLINE.
3. TAKE EACH OF THE 12 SMALLER STICKERS, ONE AT A TIME, AND STICK THEM
   ONTO THE SPACES WITH THE DARK BLUE OUTLINES.

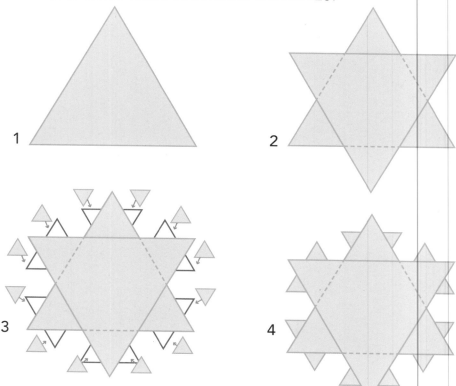

FOLLOW THE INSTRUCTIONS AND BUILD YOUR OWN BEAUTIFUL
SNOWFLAKE FROM PLANET WOCH!

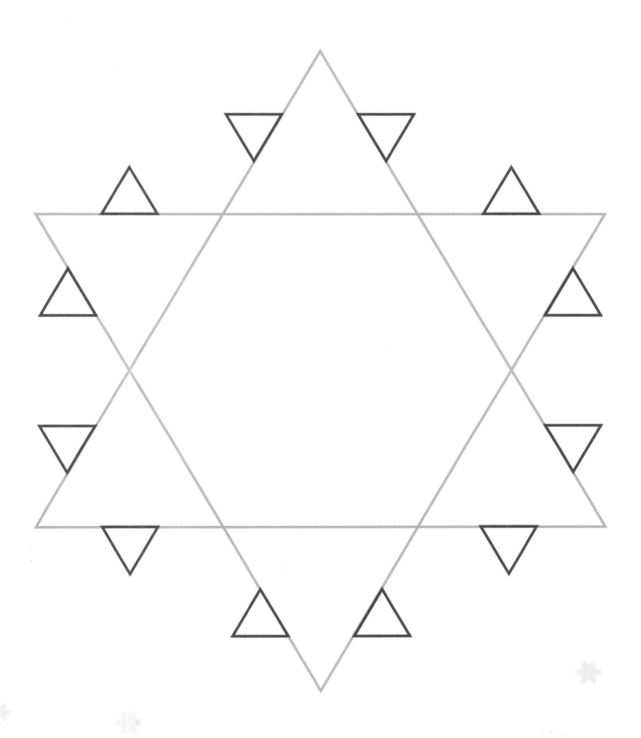

THE WORLD OF CROTON

WE HAVE REACHED THE LAST LEG OF OUR GALACTIC JOURNEY. CROTON IS AN ANCIENT PLACE INHABITED BY THE **PYTHAGORIANS**, WHO HAVE DEDICATED THEMSELVES TO STUDYING TRIANGLES, SQUARES, AND AREAS!

FIRST, OBSERVE THIS SPECIAL TRIANGLE THAT HAS A RIGHT ANGLE: IT'S CALLED A **RIGHT TRIANGLE**, AND ITS PERPENDICULAR SIDES ARE CALLED **CATHETI** (OR LEGS). THE THIRD SIDE IS CALLED THE **HYPOTENUSE**.

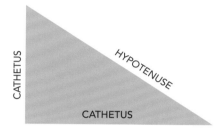

NOW YOU KNOW ABOUT RIGHT TRIANGLES. THE PYTHAGORIANS ARE EXCITED TO SHARE A HELPFUL THEOREM THAT GETS ITS NAME FROM AN ANCIENT GREEK PHILOSOPHER. JUST A MINUTE…DO YOU REMEMBER HOW TO CALCULATE THE AREA OF A SQUARE? WE SPOKE ABOUT IT ON PAGE 14.

AREA =
SIDE X SIDE

SIDE

SIDE

WE CAN ALSO SAY THAT

AREA OF SQUARE = $SIDE^2$

PYTHAGORAS' THEOREM: THE SQUARE BUILT ON THE HYPOTENUSE IS EQUAL TO THE SUM OF THE SQUARES BUILT ON THE CATHETI.

AREA H

H

AREA C1

C1

C2

AREA C2

$$H^2 = C1^2 + C2^2$$

NOW, TRY TO SOLVE THESE PROBLEMS WITH ME!
USE THE DATA YOU HAVE TO CALCULATE THE AREAS OF THE
SQUARES BELOW.

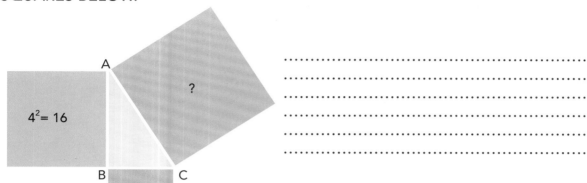

A
$4^2= 16$
?
B   C
$3^2= 9$

....
....
....
....
....
....

36 IN^2
D   ?
E   F
100 IN^2

....
....
....
....
....
....

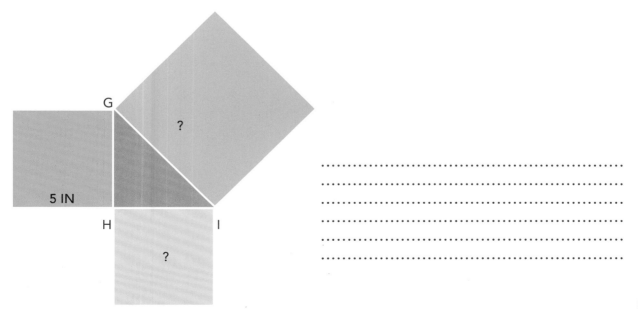

G
?
5 IN
H   I
?

....
....
....
....
....
....

SOLUTIONS

PP. 6-7: CONSTELLATIONS AND LINES

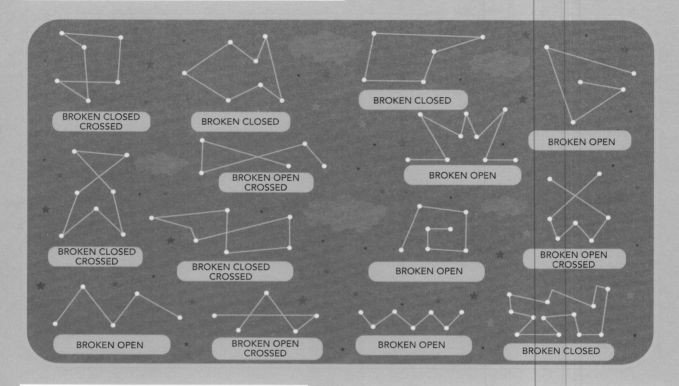

BROKEN CLOSED CROSSED

BROKEN CLOSED

BROKEN CLOSED

BROKEN OPEN

BROKEN OPEN CROSSED

BROKEN OPEN

BROKEN CLOSED CROSSED

BROKEN CLOSED CROSSED

BROKEN OPEN

BROKEN OPEN CROSSED

BROKEN OPEN

BROKEN OPEN CROSSED

BROKEN OPEN

BROKEN CLOSED

P. 9: ANGLES

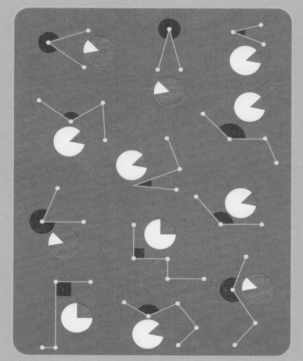

P. 11: REGULAR AND IRREGULAR POLYGONS

PP. 12–13: SIDES AND ANGLES

3 SIDES
3 ANGLES

5 SIDES
5 ANGLES

7 SIDES
7 ANGLES

9 SIDES
9 ANGLES

4 SIDES
4 ANGLES

6 SIDES
6 ANGLES

8 SIDES
8 ANGLES

10 SIDES
10 ANGLES

P. 15: AREAS

AREA=25

A=8

A=32

A=16

A=20

A=20

A=25

A=24

SIRIUS BOT AREA =70

PP. 16–17: THE GALAXIES OF LABYRINTHS

MAZE

LABYRINTH

P. 19: EULER'S THEOREM

TETRAHEDRON
FACES=4 EDGES=6 VERTICES=4
4 - 6 + 4= 2

OCTAHEDRON
FACES=8 EDGES=12 VERTICES=6
8 - 12 + 6 = 2

DODECAHEDRON
FACES=12 EDGES=30 VERTICES=20
12 - 30 + 20 = 2

ICOSAHEDRON
FACES=20 EDGES=30 VERTICES=12
20 - 30 + 12 = 2

P. 26: HOW MANY SQUARES CAN YOU SEE?

1=40 SQUARES
2=30 SQUARES
3=45 SQUARES
4=28 SQUARES

P. 27: HOW MANY TRIANGLES CAN YOU SEE?

5=20 TRIANGLES
6=27 TRIANGLES
7=42 TRIANGLES
8=24 TRIANGLES

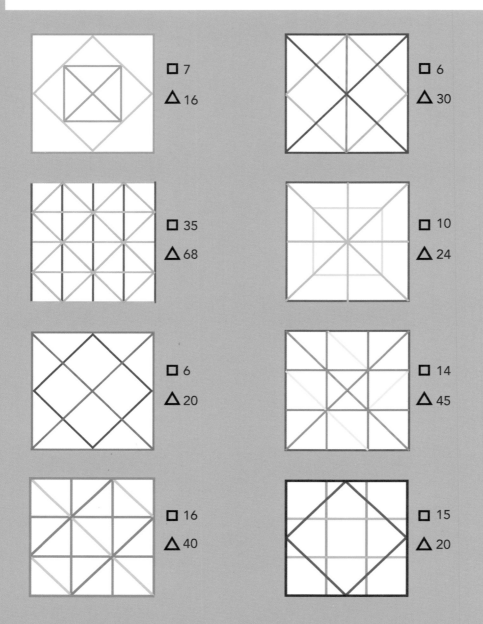

□ 7
△ 16

□ 6
△ 30

□ 35
△ 68

□ 10
△ 24

□ 6
△ 20

□ 14
△ 45

□ 16
△ 40

□ 15
△ 20

P. 31: THE PLANET-ELEVATING MACHINE

PLANETS A AND C ARE RAISED.

P. 33: TANGRAM COMETS

PP. 34-35: ASTROTAXI DISTANCES

- HOW MANY UNITS CORRESPOND TO THE MINIMUM DISTANCE BETWEEN POINTS C AND D? **17**

- THE **BLUE** ROUTE IS THE SHORTEST

- **E-F:** MINIMUM DISTANCE **15**

- **G-H:** MINIMUM DISTANCE **11**

PP. 46-47: STELLAR MAPS

P. 51: THE WORLD OF CROTON

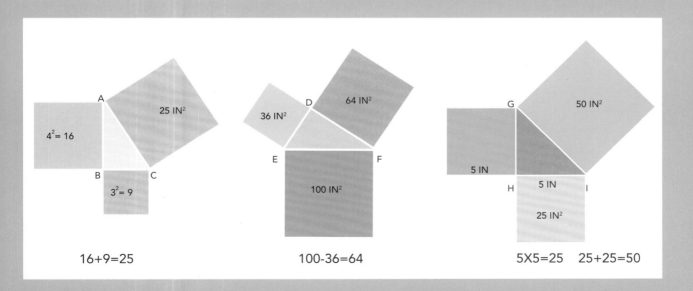

$4^2 = 16$ 25 IN²   A B C $3^2 = 9$

16+9=25

36 IN²   D   64 IN²   E F   100 IN²

100-36=64

G   50 IN²   5 IN   H 5 IN I   25 IN²

5X5=25   25+25=50

MATTIA CRIVELLINI

After graduating with a degree in information technology from the University of Bologna, Mattia went on to study cognitive sciences at Indiana University in Bloomington, Indiana. Since 2011, he has been the manager of Fosforo, the science festival of Senigallia. With the cultural organization NEXT, he organizes and plans events, shows, and conferences that showcase and promote science.

VALERIA BARATTINI

Valeria obtained a post-graduate degree in economics and management of the arts and cultural activities from the Ca' Foscari University of Venice, as well as a master's degree in standards for museum education from the Roma Tre University of Rome. She works in the fields of didactics and cultural planning. Since 2015, she has been collaborating with Fosforo, planning events and activities to promote science.

AGNESE BARUZZI

Agnese obtained a degree in graphic planning from ISIA (Superior Institute for the Arts Industries) in Urbino, Italy. Since 2001, she has been working as an illustrator and author. She has published numerous books for teenagers in Italy and abroad, collaborating with schools and libraries. In the last few years, she has enjoyed illustrating books for White Star Kids.

For special orders, quantity sales, course adoptions and corporate sales, please email the publisher at sales@mango.bz. For trade and wholesale sales, please contact Ingram Publisher Services at customer.service@ingramcontent.com or +1.800.509.4887.

Mad for Math: Make Space for Geometry
ISBN: (p) 978-1-68481-047-5
BISAC: JNF035050, JUVENILE NONFICTION / Mathematics / Geometry

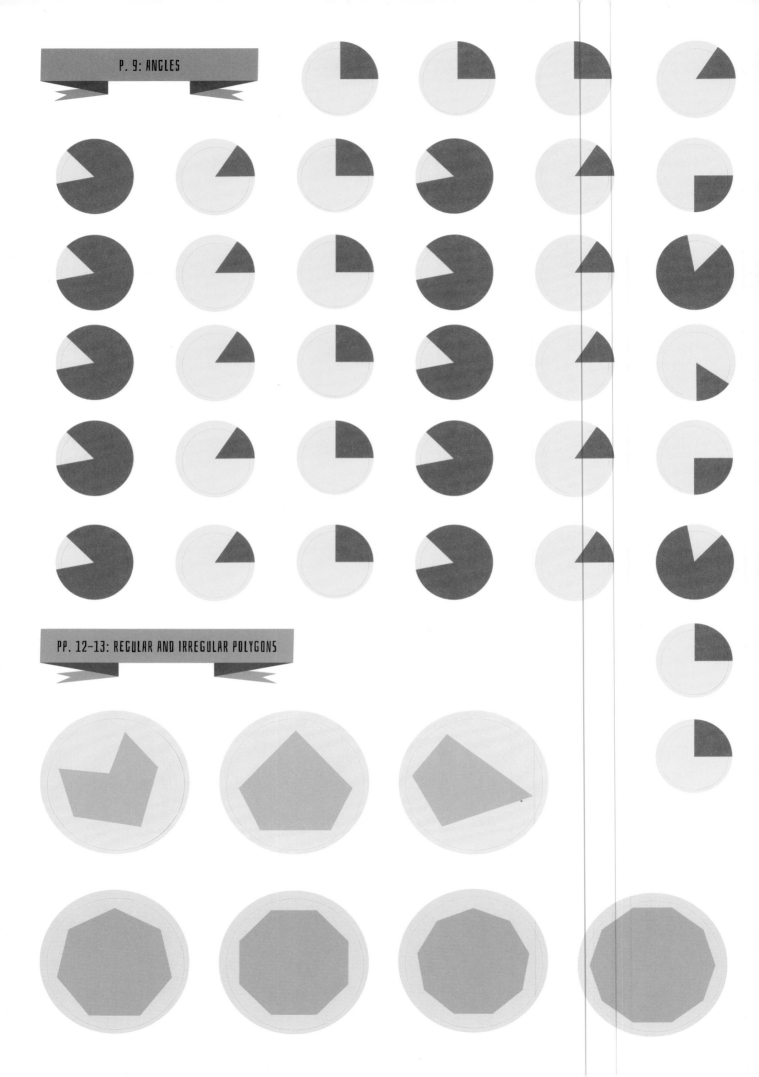

P. 9: ANGLES

PP. 12–13: REGULAR AND IRREGULAR POLYGONS

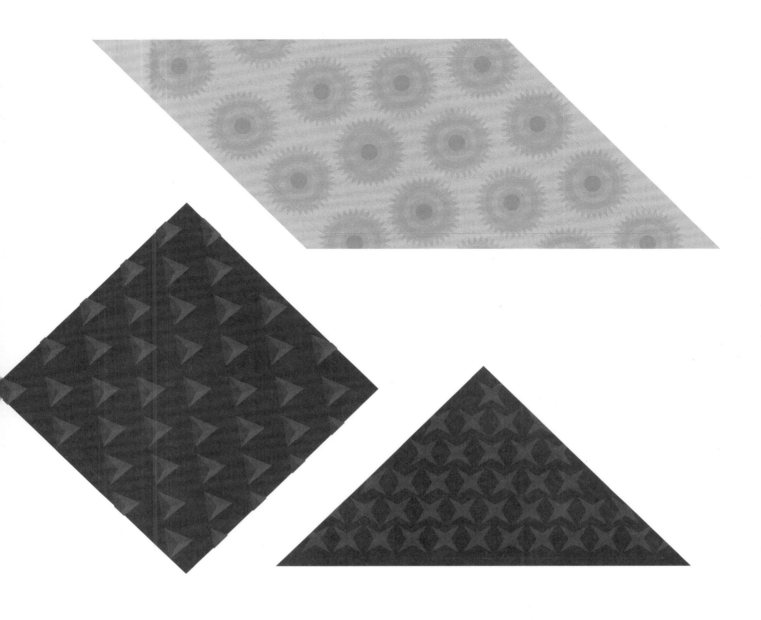

PP. 38-39: SYMMETRY AND ASTEROIDS

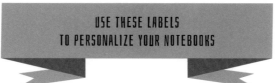

USE THESE LABELS
TO PERSONALIZE YOUR NOTEBOOKS

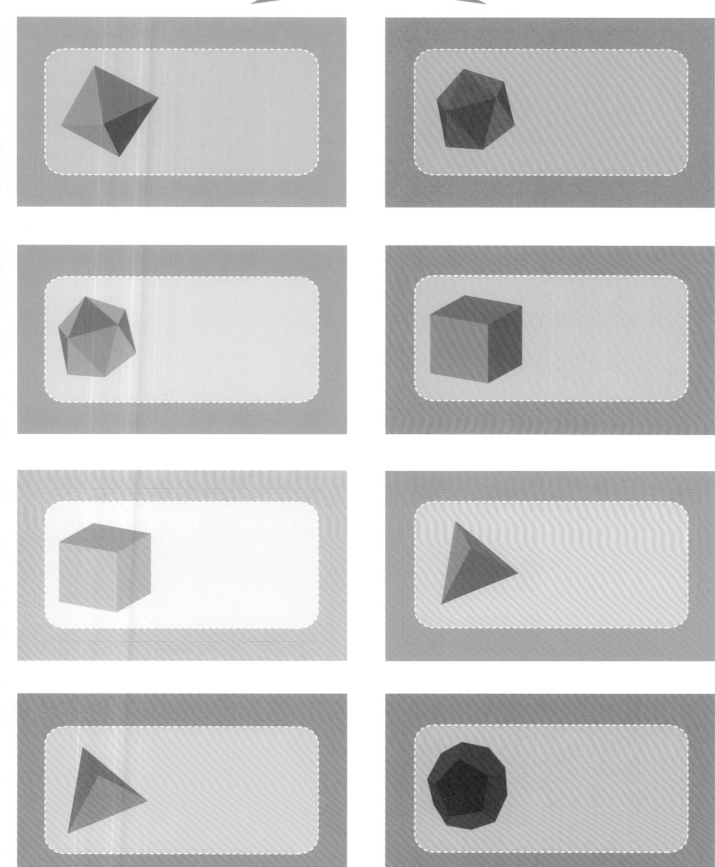